THE MYSTERY IN THE Twin Cities

Editor: Janice Baker
Assistant Editor: Susan Walworth
Cover Design: John Hanson
Content Design: Randolyn Friedlander
Photo Credits: Shutterstock.com

Gallopade International is introducing SAT words that kids need to know in
each new book that we publish. The SAT words are bold in the story. Look for
each word in the special SAT glossary. Happy Learning!

Gallopade is proud to be a member and supporter of these educational organizations
and associations:

American Booksellers Association
American Library Association
International Reading Association
National Association for Gifted Children
The National School Supply and Equipment Association
The National Council for the Social Studies
Museum Store Association
Association of Partners for Public Lands
Association of Booksellers for Children
Association for the Study of African American Life and History
National Alliance of Black School Educators

Once upon a time...

Hmm, kids keep asking me to write a mystery book. What shall I do?

Mimi

Write one about spiders!

Papa said …

Why don't you set the stories in real locations?

That's a great idea! And if I do that, I might as well choose real kids as characters in the stories! But which kids would I pick?

MiMi, PiCK ME, PiCK ME!

ME, TOO, MiMi, PiCK ME, TOO!

Christina

Grant

On the *Mystery Girl* airplane ...

I CAN FLY US anyWHERE!

Or aboard the *Mimi!*

Take me to the Forbidden City!

Or by surfboard, rickshaw, motorbike, camel ...

All great ideas! I can put a lot of history, **MYSTERY,** legend, lore, and **laughs** in the books! We can use other boys and girls in the books. It will be educational and fun!

Good stuff!

And so, Mimi, Papa, Christina, and Grant took off aboard the *Mystery Girl* and America's National Mystery Book Series—where the adventure is real and so are the characters! —was born.

START YOUR ADVENTURE TODAY!

1
MIMISODA

Grant had never worked so hard to get to a bathroom. He pulled his knee all the way to his chest and stretched his short leg. CRRRUNCH! His royal blue boot disappeared into the snow's deep white cold.

"I'm never gonna make it," he whined, wishing he had listened to his big sister, Christina. She had warned him not to drink that soda.

Still, Grant had to snicker when he remembered the conversation that started his emergency. About an hour earlier, he had said to his grandmother, "Pass me a soda, please, Mimi." Mimi always made sure her red cooler was overflowing with drinks and snacks when they made a trip. It sat securely by her feet, mostly so Grant wouldn't make himself sick on the goodies.

With the steering wheel in the steady hands of Papa, the children's grandfather, Mimi had dozed off.

"Mimi, soda!" Grant had yelled to wake her. It had only taken him a second to get his own joke and he laughed hysterically. Even Papa couldn't stifle a belly laugh that roused Mimi from her slumber.

Christina had not been as quick. "What's so funny?" she had asked.

"That's where we're going!" Grant told her. "Mimisoda!"

Christina had rolled her eyes and told him, "Funny, Grant. I showed you the state at the top of the U.S. map. It's between North Dakota and Wisconsin, remember? You know it's Minnesota, not Mimisoda! And if you drink that soda, you'll be begging for a bathroom stop."

Grant's smile faded quickly when a howling wind tossed a blast of snow into his face. He wiped his eyes with his thick, blue mittens. The rest area restroom sign was still a good 10 or 15 giant steps away at the top of a small hill. The deep snowdrift circled it like a moat around a castle. *My kingdom for a drawbridge*, he thought, wishing for something solid and flat to walk on.

To keep his mind off his urgent need for the restroom, Grant concentrated on other things as he slogged through the snow. He listed all the fun activities he'd read about in a Minnesota travel brochure. He focused on his nose, which was so cold that the end of it was beating like a heart. He remembered the annoyed look Christina had shot him when he left on his bathroom journey and told her, "Promise I'll only be a minute."

Grant understood his sister's impatience. Several months earlier, Mimi and Papa invited them to come along on this January trip to Minnesota. At their Georgia home, they marked the days off their calendar with white paper snowflakes as a reminder of the wintry adventure ahead.

Mimi, a children's mystery book writer, had an idea for a Minnesota mystery. "I need to feel the bite of winter while the story's cooking in my head," she told them. Grant knew his grandmother cooked mysteries the way other grandmothers cooked casseroles. She'd add a bit of this and a dash of that until the delicious story was done.

Mimi gave the kids an even bigger surprise when she told them they could attend a famous festival—the Saint Paul Winter Carnival, also known as "The Coolest Celebration on Earth." Grant couldn't wait for it to start!

With one last giant effort, SMLOOOCH, Grant yanked his boot out of the snow and planted it on the concrete walkway. Salt, strewn to melt the snow, glittered like broken glass. He scampered to the green metal bathroom door as fast as his frozen feet could carry him. CREEEEEAK! The heavy door groaned open. Grant slipped inside and it slammed angrily behind him. Thrilled that no one was waiting in line, he dashed into a stall.

"WHEW!" Grant sighed as he made his way to the sink. "That's what I call relief!" His voice bounced eerily off the block walls before his face turned red. *Why did I say that out loud?* he wondered, and peeked quickly under the stalls for feet. There were none. He was all alone.

The bathroom was as cold as Mimi's freezer. Grant's breath came out in puffs of smoky vapor that floated away like chilly ghosts. The late afternoon sun, shining through the bony branches of a leafless tree, cast spooky shadows on the wall.

Grant wanted to run, but he could almost hear Mimi's voice ringing in his ears— "Don't forget to wash your hands!" The warm water felt like heaven to his cold, stinging fingers. He hummed *Walkin' Through a Winter Wonderland* to calm his nerves and let his eyes follow a curious gray crack along the red concrete floor. He imagined it was a river on the red planet, Mars. Mimi often told him his imagination would either make him a fine writer some day or get him into loads of trouble! So far, it had mostly been the latter.

Just as his imaginary Martian river reached the bathroom door, KA-POW! The door blasted open in a blinding ball of flashing fire.

Before Grant could move, an icy snowball clobbered him in the neck, and then exploded on the red concrete like a bag of spilled diamonds. Panicked, Grant thought, *I haven't even met anyone in Minnesota and already someone's out to get me!*

2
MISSING MEDALLION!

Grant gasped for air. His lungs crackled like ice cubes in sweet tea. His legs, plowing through the snow, begged for a break. But he was afraid to slow down. Someone or some*thing* had attacked him in the bathroom!

As he neared the parking lot, Grant noticed a hulking black minivan that hadn't been there when he left. *Could it be his attacker? Were Mimi, Papa, and Christina OK?*

Grant was relieved to spot Christina waiting beside the car. "Well, that was the longest minute I ever lived through," she said sarcastically as he stumbled toward her.

"You'll...never believe...what happened," he said, working hard to force the words out of his frozen throat.

"You'll never believe what's gonna happen to you if we don't get back on the road," Christina said.

"But, you don't understand!" Grant said. "There was fire...and ice!"

"Another tall tale," Christina sighed. "You're the only person I know who goes to the bathroom and finds a fantastic story!"

Before Grant had a chance to say more, the black van let out a loud honk. He spun around just in time to see someone wearing a purple parka dive into it. Its tires flung a rooster tail of gravel and snow into the air before it whizzed onto the highway.

"I wish we'd brought the *Mystery Girl*," Papa said impatiently when Christina and Grant crawled into the toasty warm car. "We'd have been there hours ago." He was talking about his trusty red and white airplane that had taken them on adventures all over the world.

"Just think of the beautiful sights we would have missed," Mimi scolded him.

"Well, if we don't make up for lost time," he said, "I'm afraid we'll miss seeing Chester."

Papa's friend Chester Calhoun lived in Saint Paul, Minnesota. He had promised to meet them at the Saint Paul Hotel and show them around. Like Papa, he was a pilot. He and his wife, Shirley, had used their plane recently to help the victims of a terrible earthquake on the island of Haiti.

Grant was exhausted from his bathroom trek. He knew Papa and Christina were in no mood to hear about his ordeal. He rubbed his neck. Anyone could've thrown a snowball into the bathroom. But what about the flash of fire?

"Look!" Mimi exclaimed as they clickety-clacked across a bridge. "We're crossing the Mississippi!"

"The Mississippi?" Grant asked. "What's it doing way up here?"

Christina sighed. "The Mississippi River is the largest river system in the United States," she explained, sounding like a fourth grade textbook. "It begins in Minnesota and runs all the way to the Gulf of Mexico."

"Yes, ma'am," Mimi agreed. "Saint Paul got its start as a busy river port and eventually became the capital of Minnesota!"

When Papa pulled up to the historic Saint Paul Hotel, the sun's last rays were sliding down its yellow brick exterior and lounging on the snow-covered lawn.

Mimi told them the grand hotel was built in 1910. "Presidents, movie stars, and even kings and queens have stayed here," she said excitedly.

"And soon they'll say that Grant stayed here!" Grant chirped.

Inside, the lobby teemed with tourists bundled in puffy jackets. Christina elbowed Grant and whispered, "They look like marshmallows looking for S'mores!"

"Yeah!" Grant agreed.

"There he is!" Papa said when he spotted Chester. He waved his black cowboy hat in the air. Just like Papa, Chester was tall and wore faded jeans and cowboy boots.

"Must be a pilot thing," Christina said when she noticed their similar fashion choice.

Chester's wife, Shirley, was a pretty lady with a kind smile. She gave Christina and Grant robust hugs, even though they'd never met her before.

"It's great to have you in our neck of the woods!" Chester said. "Especially Christina and Grant. We hear they're great at solving mysteries and we need their help."

Christina and Grant exchanged surprised looks. "What's up?" Christina asked.

"While we were in Haiti," Shirley said, "we flew children who'd lost their parents to an orphanage. Some were picked up later by family members, but there were two little boys..."

Chester continued, "They're twins. They don't have any family. Since Shirley and I don't have any children, we'd like to adopt them." He yanked a black leather wallet from his back pocket. Gingerly, he pulled out a photo of two little boys about 3 years old. Black hair hung in ringlets around faces the color of coffee.

Grant was amazed at their big smiles considering all they'd been through.

"That's wonderful!" Papa said. "How can we help?"

"Adopting a child from a foreign county is expensive," Chester explained. "Adopting twins is twice as expensive, so we need to raise more money."

"We could open a lemonade stand, or I guess in this weather, a hot chocolate stand," Grant suggested.

Chester and Shirley laughed. "That's a great idea, Grant," Chester said. "But we've got another plan. The Winter Carnival lasts 10 days and includes more than 100 winter sports and entertainment events in different places around Saint Paul. But one of the biggest events is the hunt for the Winter Carnival Medallion. It's like a scavenger hunt. The finder can win thousands of dollars!"

"The *Pioneer Press*, a local newspaper, prints clues," Shirley said. "It's called the '*Pioneer Press* Treasure Hunt.'"

Christina smiled at Grant. "Clues are our business," she said.

Mimi shook her head. She knew that clues usually got them knee-deep in trouble. She was about to lecture them when a woman's shrill scream made everyone in the lobby freeze like kids in a game of tag.

"Oh no!" the woman yelled into her cell phone. She closed the phone and shared the bad news. "The Winter Carnival Medallion has been stolen!"

Christina and Grant exchanged knowing glances. They had more than a scavenger hunt on their hands. This was a real mystery!

3
A KOOKY KREWE

Chester and Shirley couldn't hide their disappointment. "It was supposed to be hidden after the Winter Carnival opening ceremony," Chester said. "I guess we don't have a chance at that prize money now."

"Can't they just make another medallion to hide?" Grant asked.

"If it were that easy," Shirley explained, "there would be counterfeit medallions floating around everywhere. Anyone could turn one in and claim the prize money."

"But what about the twins?" Christina asked.

"We'll find a way," Chester said, wrapping his arm around Shirley's shoulders. "It just may take longer than we had planned."

"Maybe this will give you time to learn about raising twins," Papa said.

"No worries there," Shirley said. "We've got lots of experience with twins."

"We surely do," Chester agreed. "Our next door neighbor has twin boys. They've spent so much time at our house, we practically raised them. We love them like our own sons."

"Sure are a lot of twins around," Grant said. He whirled around to face his sister. "I'm glad Christina's not my twin. I'd never want to look like that!"

Christina flicked her long brown hair over her shoulder. "You're just jealous," she told Grant. "That curly blonde hair makes you look like a Q-tip!"

"Stop it, you two," Mimi scolded. "You shouldn't be surprised there are a lot of twins here. After all, this is the Twin Cities!"

Grant looked confused. "I thought we were in Saint Paul," he said.

"We are," Mimi agreed. "But Saint Paul has a twin—Minneapolis."

Grant snickered. "Are you sure it's not MIMI-apolis?" he asked.

"*Still* not funny, Grant," Christina said. "Will we get to see both cities, Mimi?"

"I sure hope so," Mimi said and gave Chester a pleading look.

"Of course!" Chester said. "I've got a tour planned that will make King Boreas proud."

"Who's King Boreas?" Grant asked.

"He's the powerful King of the Winds," Chester said. "During his travels throughout the world, he found a winter paradise named Minnesota. He declared Saint Paul the capital of his winter playground."

"Awesome!" Grant said. "Does he have a throne and everything?"

"Whoa!" Papa said with his best cowboy voice. "You've got more splainin' to do, Chester."

Chester chuckled. "King Boreas is just a fun legend," he said. "Each year, someone is chosen to be King Boreas, but he's not a real king. In fact, an entire royal family is chosen each year, including a Queen of Snows and a prince and princess for each of the four winds."

"Look!" Christina said. "The hotel has a floor show!"

A kooky-looking character lumbered through the lobby. He wore a red running suit. A red cape flapped behind him. A ridge across the top of his red cap reminded Christina of a rooster comb. He glanced their way through big, black, bug-eyed goggles.

"That's not an entertainer," Shirley said. "He's a member of the Vulcan Krewe—a follower of The Fire King—Vulcanus Rex. It's another fun Winter Carnival tradition. The Vulcan Krewe pretends to battle King Boreas to drive winter out of Saint Paul and bring back the warm weather."

Curious, Christina watched the Vulcan carefully. He yanked off a long black glove to push the elevator UP button. Something fell out and fluttered to the floor. The Vulcan didn't notice, but Christina did.

Grant, however, focused on something else. Someone wearing a purple parka was getting on the elevator too!

4
LUCY WHO?

"We've got to talk," Christina whispered to Grant when they finished supper with Chester and Shirley in the hotel restaurant.

"Did you see?" Grant asked.

"Yes!" Christina said. "I've got it in my pocket!"

Grant looked puzzled. "What?" he asked.

"Follow my lead," Christina instructed. She smiled sweetly at Mimi and asked in her most polite voice. "Mimi, may we be excused? We'd like to find some interesting historical plaques to read."

"I don't want to read any boring old plaques!" Grant whispered.

Christina kicked him under the table to make him hush.

"Ouch!" he yelped.

Mimi didn't notice. "That's fine," she said. "Just don't go too far away!"

"Meet us back at the room!" Papa said.

"We will!" Christina said as they scrambled out of their chairs and raced from the restaurant.

In the lobby, Christina punched the elevator UP button. "Great," she said impatiently. "It's on the top floor."

Grant rubbed his ankle. "What'd you have to kick me for?" he asked. "And please explain how you have a person in a purple parka in your pocket?"

"What on earth are you rambling on about, Grant?" she asked, annoyed.

"When I asked if you saw it, you said you had it in your pocket!" he exclaimed. "I was talking about the person in the purple parka who got on the elevator. I saw the same purple parka at the rest area. I've got a hunch that's who attacked me in the bathroom with the fire and ice."

"Oh, hunch, punch," Christina said. "Do you still expect me to believe that story? Besides, I'm sure there are lots of people in Minnesota with purple parkas."

Christina stuffed her hand into her jeans pocket and pulled out a tightly folded piece of paper. She slapped it into Grant's hand. "I was talking about this," she said.

Grant shook the note open. It said:

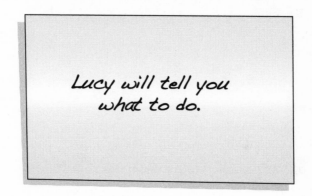

Lucy will tell you
what to do.

5
COATS, CAPS, AND CONFUSION

"Are we going to Lucy's room?" Grant asked.

A loud huff escaped Christina's lips. "I don't have a clue who or where Lucy is, Grant. I wanted to get away from the grownups. You know how Mimi feels about us getting involved in these things."

"Then why'd you push the UP button?" Grant asked.

Christina wondered the same thing. "I don't know," she answered. "Let's explore the hotel. Maybe we'll stumble on another clue."

As the elevator flashed the floor numbers on its descent, Christina's mind raced. *Tales of kings and Vulcans...a valuable missing medallion...thousands of angry and upset people, including Chester and Shirley, who had hoped to find it.... Was the Lucy note a clue or a coincidence? What were they getting mixed up in? What if the kooky Vulcan Krewe member just realized his note was missing? What if he was headed down on the elevator?*

Christina's heart thumped. *What if*...DING! The elevator doors whooshed open. A person in a purple parka bolted out. WHAM! Grant didn't know what hit him. But as his feet flew into the air and he rolled onto the floor, he saw the purple parka. He grabbed a sleeve and pulled with all his might.

"I caught him!" Grant hollered. "Help me, Christina!"

Christina was horrified. "Grant, stop it!" she commanded, pulling her brother off his victim. A frightened, freckle-faced boy looked at Grant with blue eyes as big as moon pies and dashed off.

"What'd you do that for?" Grant asked in a voice so furious spit came out with his words. "I'm sure that's who attacked me. I was gonna make him talk!"

"Well, now you're the one in trouble," Christina said and pointed to the purple parka in Grant's hands. "You're a parka thief. We've gotta find that kid and return his coat."

"How will we find him without his purple coat?" Grant asked.

"Easy," Christina said. She was proud of her keen observation. "He's wearing a white cap with a purple stripe across it."

Christina and Grant scurried through the grand Saint Paul Hotel lobby looking for the white cap. They padded across colorful carpets. They clipped-clopped over marble floors that reflected the dazzling chandeliers above them. They spun around the cool marble columns as if they were Maypoles. Finally, in a cozy corner near a fireplace, Christina spotted the cap. The kid was snuggled in a chair, calmly reading a book!

"At least he doesn't look upset," Christina whispered to Grant. "Now go and apologize."

Grant tiptoed behind the chair and tapped the kid's shoulder. "Excuse me," he said. "I'm sorry I attacked you when you came off the elevator." Grant sheepishly held up the parka.

Big blue eyes looked at Grant with a puzzled expression. "I think you're confused," the kid said. "You didn't attack me."

Now Grant looked puzzled. "Sure I did," he said. "Here's your coat to prove it!"

The kid examined the tag inside and said, "Nope. Not my coat. See, the tag clearly says this belongs to Jim."

"So, you're telling me you're not Jim?" Grant asked.

The kid slowly removed the cap. Long, silky-blonde hair spilled out!

Grant and Christina had a feeling they'd made a big mistake!

6
PURPLE PARKA PARTNERS

Grant's mouth dropped like a rock and his face turned redder than Mimi's favorite lipstick. "Why, you're not a boy!" he said. "I tackled a girl!"

"Thanks for noticing!" the girl said. "My name's Julie. But you never tackled me."

Before Grant could say another word, a yell echoed among the marble columns. "That's him!" shouted a boy, also in a white cap. "He's the one who stole my coat!"

Grant couldn't deny it. He was holding the evidence in his hand! "Oh boy," he muttered and looked helplessly at Christina. He hoped she could help get him out of this mess.

The boy marched up to Grant and demanded, "Why'd you do it?"

His father said, "Now slow down a minute, Jim. Maybe he's got a perfectly good reason for taking your coat."

Grant looked at the boy, then back at Julie, and sighed. "I'm so confused!" he said.

Julie burst into a laugh that bounced around the lobby like a beach ball. "Looks like another case of mistaken identity."

"Oh, I get it!" Christina said. "You two are twins!"

Grant slapped his forehead. "More twins!" he whined. "And they're identical!"

"A boy and a girl can't be identical twins," Julie explained. "We're fraternal twins, but we do look a lot alike."

Jim was impatient. "That still doesn't explain why you stole my parka!" he huffed.

"I'm sorry," Grant stammered. "I thought you were someone else."

"See, Jim," the father said. "Just a great big mix-up. I told you not to jump to conclusions. My name's James Snowdon," he told Christina and Grant. "You kids are close to the same age. Why don't you all get to know each other? I need to tend to the dogs."

The twins watched their father until he was out of sight and then looked awkwardly at Christina and Grant. "So who did you think I was?" Jim finally asked Grant.

Grant quickly recounted his encounter at the rest area. Jim and Julie exchanged embarrassed looks. "I'm afraid that was us," Julie said.

"Both of you?" Grant asked.

"It's a game we play when we're on our way to the Winter Festival each year," she said. "Jim pretends to be in the Fire King's legion, helping the Fire King get rid of winter."

"You mean Vulcanus Rex?" Christina asked.

"Yeah," Julie said. "He has this toy torch that flashes like fire."

Jim grinned. "It looks real," he bragged.

"I pretend I'm King Boreas' Queen of Snows," Julie said. "I throw snowballs to fight off the spring. I'm afraid you got caught in the middle."

"Told you I was attacked by fire and ice!" Grant told Christina triumphantly.

"What are your names?" Julie asked, realizing she hadn't officially met them.

Christina and Grant introduced themselves and plopped on a sofa. Christina sorted out the situation. Grant had said a kid in a purple parka got on the elevator with the kooky character dressed in red.

"Is there any chance your dad is a member of the Vulcan Krewe?" Christina asked.

"Gosh no," Julie said. "He's a dog musher!"

Grant was horrified. He gulped and asked cautiously, "He smushes dogs?"

Jim and Julie roared with laughter. "No, he's a dogsled driver," Jim said. "He brings his team of dogs here every year to compete in the dogsled competition. It's one of the Winter Carnival events."

"Whew!" said Grant, relieved. "We've already got a big mystery to solve. I don't want to have to rescue dogs from being smushed."

Christina shot Grant a "don't say another word," look. But it was too late. Julie and Jim had already heard the "M" word.

"Your mystery wouldn't have anything to do with the missing medallion, would it?" Jim asked.

Christina twisted her shoelaces nervously. She wasn't sure she could trust these mischievous twins. On the other hand, she'd never been to Saint Paul before, and could use some extra help. She looked at Grant. He was usually a good judge of character.

"I think we can trust them," Grant said.

Christina was about to tell them about the odd clue she'd found when a young man wearing a dark gray business suit rushed into the lobby. He felt frantically around chair cushions as if he'd lost something very important. Flustered, he eyed the kids suspiciously before storming away.

Christina had seen someone in a red running suit drop the note. *But what if he had changed clothes? What if this man in the dark gray business suit and the man in the red running suit were the same person?*

7
PEANUTS IN RICE

Christina peered over her shoulder to make sure no one was watching them. She handed the "Lucy" note to the twins.

"Any ideas about what it could mean?" she asked.

Jim shook his head. But Julie pressed her finger to her lips as if coaxing out a thought. "Do you guys like cartoons?" she asked.

"Sure!" Grant said. "I'd love to watch some right now!"

Christina was always amazed at how Grant's mind could switch from one thing to another so quickly—like changing television channels.

"No, Grant," Julie said. "I wasn't suggesting that we watch TV. Have you ever seen the old Peanuts cartoons? They were made in the 1960s when our parents were little kids. It's also a newspaper cartoon strip."

Grant rested his chin in his hand and drummed his chubby cheek with his fingers. *"Peanuts...Peanuts..."* he said, thinking hard. "It's not ringing a bell."

"Oh for Pete's sake," Christina said. "Ever hear of Charlie Brown?"

"Of course!" Grant said. "I love *A Charlie Brown Christmas*. Mimi loves it too. We always snuggle on her big comfy couch and drink hot chocolate when we watch it together."

Grant blushed when he realized he sounded like a baby. The red started on his neck and crept up his face like red Kool-Aid spilled on a white rug. "What I meant to say was—that's what we did when I was a little kid," he explained. "Snoopy was our favorite character. Mimi liked Lucy too, but I think she's annoying."

"What did you just say, Grant?" Christina asked.

"I said that Lucy's annoying," he answered. "Come to think of it, she's a lot like you sometimes!"

"Lucy!" Christina said. "Julie, are you telling us that Charlie Brown's friend, Lucy, has something to do with this clue?"

"Just a thought," Julie said. "She was the first Lucy who popped in my head, and Charles Schulz is from Saint Paul."

"Charles Schulz?" Grant asked.

"He created *Peanuts*," Jim said. "Even I know that."

"Charles Schulz was born in Minneapolis and raised in Saint Paul," Julie explained. "He got his start as a cartoonist at the *Saint Paul Pioneer Press*."

"The newspaper that sponsors the medallion search?" Christina asked.

"Yep," Julie said. "Mr. Schulz's family placed bronze statues of all the *Peanuts* characters in Rice Park in his honor. I was just thinking..."

"You were just thinking that the statue of Lucy in Rice Park might hold the answer to this clue!" Christina said, finishing her sentence.

"How can we go poking around Rice Park at night?" Grant asked. "Besides, we promised Mimi and Papa we wouldn't go far. If we get caught, we might be turned into rice pudding."

Jim snickered. "Or Rice-a-Roni," he suggested.

"Or rice cakes!" Grant said.

"Enough, you guys!" Christina said. "How far is it to Rice Park?"

"It's right out the front door of the hotel!" Julie exclaimed.

"Well, I bet there are some interesting historical plaques out there!" Christina said. "And technically, we won't be leaving the hotel—just getting some air in the front yard!"

Christina knew that "getting air" was an understatement when she stepped out into the bone-chilling night. "I think someone left the refrigerator door open," she said.

"I th-th-th-think I'd like t-t-t-to go in a refrigerator to w-w-w-warm up," Grant said through chattering chompers.

Jim pulled his fur-rimmed hood over his head.

"The problem is your coats," Jim observed. "They're not right for this weather. You need parkas like we have."

"I hope they don't have to be p-p-purple," Grant muttered under his breath.

Even in the dim glow of the park lights, Christina could see that Rice Park was a gorgeous place. She regretted they hadn't arrived early enough to explore it in daylight.

"Did this park get its name because the winter snow makes it looks like a big bowl of rice?" Grant asked.

"Of course not," Christina said. "I read about it in a brochure at the hotel. It was named for Henry Mower Rice. He was Minnesota's first U.S. senator. It's been a public square since the mid 1800s."

"That would be some old rice," Grant said, still stuck on the rice bowl theory. "It would be all moldy by now for sure!"

Christina ignored her brother's silly comment and gazed around the park. She gasped in wonder. A well-lit castle, complete with blue-topped turrets and a clock tower, loomed over the shadowy landscape.

Grant spotted it too. "Is that where King Boreas lives?" he asked.

Jim and Julie laughed. "That's the Landmark Center. It was built in 1902 as a Federal courthouse and post office for the entire upper Midwest of the United States."

"That's the fanciest post office I've ever seen," Grant said.

"It's not a post office anymore," Julie explained. "My dad said they planned to tear the old building down in the 1970s, but a group of Saint Paul citizens worked to save it. Now, it's a place for plays, dance performances, concerts, and things like that."

"Tell him the cool part!" Jim begged.

"Oh yeah," Julie continued. "In the 1930s, there were a lot of famous gangsters tried in the courthouse. One of them was a member of the famous Ma Barker's gang. His name was Alvin 'Creepy' Karpis."

"I'll bet his ghost is still up there," Jim said in a spooky voice. He opened his eyes wide, held his hands straight out and walked like a zombie. "He's probably watching us out of one of those high windows right now!"

Grant laughed. He was glad to see that Jim had his sense of humor. Christina shuddered. Only this time it wasn't from the cold!

8
GRANT LOVES LUCY

Christina tried to shake the thoughts of "Creepy's" eyes following their every move. Still, she kept glancing over her shoulder, just in case. They hadn't walked far when she noticed a distinct clop, clop, clop behind them.

Christina froze. "Shhhhh!!!" she said. Through the shadowy trees, she spied a man who had stopped too. He was wearing a suit and had a trench coat swung over his arm. He was holding his hat in his hand.

"It's him," Christina whispered in panic. "I'll bet that's the businessman who was snooping around the lobby. He's followed us into the park. He's after the clue!"

Grant shuffled closer to his sister and peered into the shadows. "I s-s-see h-h-him," Grant said. He's staring right at us! Let's run!"

Grant took off in a flash, but Julie grabbed his coat so that he was only spinning his feet on the slick pavement. Julie and Jim hee-hawed like donkeys at a square dance!

Christina couldn't believe her eyes. They were helping the man in the business suit! She and Grant had been double crossed!

Christina glared at Julie. "Let him go!" she ordered.

When Julie saw the rage in Christina's eyes, she let go of Grant's coat. FLOP! He flew into a snow bank beside the sidewalk.

"Hey!" Julie said. "What's wrong?"

"We made a big mistake trusting you," Christina said. "You're with him, aren't you?"

"Christina," Julie said, trying hard to wipe the grin off her face. "You need to take another look at the man following you."

Christina slowly turned to look at the man again. He hadn't moved a muscle.

Julie stifled another snicker. "See!" she said. "It's only Mr. Fitzgerald."

"Who's Mr. Fitzgerald?" Grant said, brushing the snow off his coat.

"F. Scott Fitzgerald," Julie said. "A lot of people say he was one of America's greatest writers."

Christina was glad it was too dark for the others to see her blush. "Oh, I see now," she said. "It's a statue!"

"I bet there's a plaque," Grant said. "You told Mimi we were going to read historical plaques, so we'd better keep our promise."

"Good idea," Christina agreed.

The kids crunched across the snow to the statue. "It says he was born in Saint Paul and wrote a book called *The Great Gatsby*," Grant said. "I've told Mimi she should write a book called *The Great Grant*, but she hasn't gotten around to it yet."

"Do you know who he was named after?" Jim asked. "Francis Scott Key, the man who wrote the "Star-Spangled Banner"! They were distant cousins."

"That's pretty cool," Grant remarked. He reached for the statue's hand. "Great to meet you, Mr. Fitzgerald!"

When the kids got back on the main path, Christina suddenly remembered something. "I may have been confused about the statue, but I did hear footsteps behind us," she said.

"Maybe it was them," Jim said, pointing. A young couple snuggled on one of the park benches. When the boy kissed the girl, Grant had seen enough. "That's gross!" he cried.

"So which way to Lucy?" Christina asked.

Julie waved for them to follow her. Powdery snowflakes, floating down like feathers after a pillow fight, frosted the walk.

A few steps later, Grant spotted a bronze figure of a boy leaning against a tree. "He looks familiar!" he said.

"That's Charlie Brown," Jim explained, "and that's Snoopy resting on his lap."

Soon, the kids rounded a circular fountain. Water sprays that would tinkle cheerfully in warm weather circled a bronze statue like icy spiders waiting for a meal.

"Oh, I see her!" Christina said when they finally spotted Lucy. She was lying on her stomach with her arms propped on the piano of another *Peanuts* character, Schroeder.

"Wait!" Christina ordered, when they started toward the statue. She pointed out footprints that led to Lucy and kept going on the other side of a low wall. "We're not Lucy's first visitors tonight," she said. "Keep your eyes open!"

"This is my favorite *Peanuts* statue," Julie remarked, patting Lucy's cold, metal head. "It's so sweet the way she loves Schroeder."

"That lovey-dovey stuff makes me sick!" Grant said.

"You're just scared of girls," Jim said. "I bet you don't even have the courage to kiss a statue of a girl."

"That's silly," Grant said.

"Then go ahead," Jim coaxed. "If you don't have a yellow chicken liver, why don't you give the statue a kiss? I dare you!"

"Stop it, Jim!" Julie scolded. "You know what will happen...Grant, don't!" she yelled. It was too late! Grant had already licked his lips and was planting a kiss on Lucy's bronze cheek!

"AIEEEEEEEE!!!!!" Grant hollered through lips that froze instantly to the statue. Christina, examining the statue for clues, was annoyed. "Be quiet, Grant!" she said. "Someone might be watching."

Grant hollered again. "AIEEEEEEE!!!!"

"SHHHHH!" Christina said, as she pulled at a piece of paper wedged beneath Lucy's hand. "I think I found something!"

"Christina, we have a serious problem," Julie said.

"What?" Christina asked.

"His lips are stuck to the statue!" Julie cried.

Grant pulled at his lips. They stretched like fleshy rubber bands, but refused to let go. His eyes bulged out in terror and he mumbled words they couldn't understand.

Christina didn't know whether to laugh or cry. "What in the world...?" she said.

Jim was about to explain when Julie held up her hand and said, "What's that?"

They couldn't see anyone, but footsteps headed their way at a fast clip.

What do we do now? Christina thought.

9
GRANT'S LIPSTICK

Clop, clop, clippety clip, clop, clop clippety clip. Christina heard more than one set of footsteps. She strained to see who was coming, but couldn't make them out.

"Grant, come on!" she pleaded. "We don't have much time!"

All Grant could get out was "AIEEEEEEE!"

"We need some warm water to pour over his lips!" Julie said.

The footsteps were getting closer.

Christina looked around hopelessly. There was no chance of finding warm water out here, and there was no way she'd leave her brother alone.

"Why don't you two run," Christina suggested. "If that's trouble coming, there's no reason for you to face it too."

"No way," Julie said. "We're partners!"

Jim nodded in agreement. "Partners!" he said.

The footsteps stopped suddenly. "This is it," Christina said. "I think they must see us." She moved closer to Grant. If anybody got to her little brother, they'd have to go through her first.

Deep laughter and shrill cackles combined in the night air. "Would you look at that," a familiar voice boomed. "Looks like somebody lost a bet."

Christina could make out a cowboy hat emerging from the shadows. "Papa!" she cried.

Another man stepped from the shadows. It was Jim and Julie's dad, Mr. Snowdon.

"That you, Dad?" Jim asked.

"Yes," Mr. Snowdon answered. "When I got back from checking on the dogs, I couldn't find you anywhere. Then I met Mimi and Papa looking for their grandkids. I suspected we'd find you all together."

"Sorry, Dad," Julie said. "We got carried away telling Christina and Grant about Rice Park."

"I can see that," he said. "Now, let's see if we can end Grant's love affair with Lucy!"

"AIEEEEEEE!" Grant squealed helplessly.

Mimi, who tried to control her giggles while she consoled Grant, had set her cup of coffee on top of Lucy's bronze head.

"Mind if I borrow your coffee, Mimi?" Mr. Snowdon asked.

"Help yourself," Mimi replied.

Mr. Snowdon gently poured the warm coffee around Grant's mouth. POP! With a sound like a stopper yanked from a bathtub, Grant was free.

"Yuk!" Grant sputtered. "I hate caw-ee!"

"Why are you talking so funny?" Christina asked.

"My liss hu't!" Grant mumbled.

"Your lips hurt?" Christina asked.

"Yesssss!" Grant cried.

"Keep plenty of lip balm on them and they'll be good as new in a few days," Mr. Snowdon said, and then turned to Jim with a frown. "I suspect you had something to do with this."

"Aw, Dad," Jim said. "Everybody has to fall for that gag at least once!"

"You've fallen for it several times," Julie said with a laugh.

"Why'd I stick?" Grant managed to ask.

"The statue's temperature was below freezing," Papa said.

"Below 32 degrees?" Christina asked, amazed.

"That's right," Papa said. "The saliva on Grant's lips froze instantly when it touched the statue."

"I'll never kiss anudder gull as long as I lif," Grant said.

"That better not include me!" Mimi said with a laugh. "Now let's get in out of this cold and find some hot chocolate and then some nice warm beds! We've got lots to do and see tomorrow!"

Christina patted the note in her pocket. In the commotion she hadn't had time to read it. Mentally, she added one more thing to Mimi's list—*and mysteries to solve*.

10
UP WITH THE BIRDS

Christina wriggled restlessly under her fluffy down comforter and waited impatiently for sunlight to peek through the crack between the drapes. She had relived their first day in Minnesota over and over.

She thought about two little boys in Haiti, desperately waiting to live with Chester and Shirley. She wondered why someone would want to steal the Winter Carnival medallion and dash the dreams of those who wanted to win the prize money. And mostly, Christina thought about the coincidence of seeing the man dressed in the red Vulcan Krewe suit drop a note that turned out to be a clue. *Was he taking the note to someone, or had someone given the note to him? Was he really a*

Vulcan Krewe member or was he only dressed like one? And what about that young man who was so desperate to find something in the lobby? Did he have anything to do with this mess of a mystery? Had he been looking for the note?

The bed suddenly felt like quicksand and Christina felt that she was sinking fast in the **minutia** of this mystery. Her head felt hot. Christina slid her fingers under her pillow. The sheet underneath it was smooth. She grasped the note she'd found on the Lucy statue. She had hoped sleeping on it might drive its meaning into her brain during the night, but it had not. She quickly flipped her pillow and laid her head on the cool side. It was something she often did during hot Georgia summers.

Thanks to his own ordeal, Grant didn't realize Christina had found a note. She had decided he'd be in a more helpful mood after a good night's sleep.

Finally, rays of sun as sharp as spears stabbed Christina's eyes. She bounded out of bed and slid her pink fuzzy sleeping socks over the carpet to get a good static charge.

"Time to get up, Grant!" she said as she shuffled over to his bed. Zap! She touched his ear to release her static charge.

"Owww!" Grant yelped.

He sat up and gazed blankly at Christina. With his wide eyes and the tufts of hair sticking up on each side of his head, he reminded her of a surprised owl. Then there were the lips...

As soon as they returned to the hotel the night before, Mimi had coated Grant's lips with a thick coat of lip balm. Unfortunately, the only tube she had was tinted with her favorite color—red.

"You look like an old lady owl!" Christina crowed.

Papa opened the door from their adjoining room and said, "Well, look who's up with the birds this morning!"

Christina, laughing hysterically, pointed at Grant. "Bird is a good word choice, Papa," she said.

Papa cleared his throat dramatically. Christina knew a joke was coming.

"Better comb your hair and wash that beak before breakfast," Papa said. "Unless you'll be having worms instead of pancakes!"

Grant opened his mouth in a cavernous yawn and flapped his arms like wings. "Hooo! Hooo!" he hooted. "Who wouldn't like a plate of warm worms bathed in maple syrup?"

Christina gagged. Grant grinned. He'd gotten the last laugh after all.

In the hotel restaurant, Julie and Jim had saved places at their table for Grant and Christina. Mimi and Papa sat with Mr. and Mrs. Snowdon and enjoyed another laugh about the previous night's events.

After the kids wolfed down their stacks of wild blueberry pancakes, Julie could stand it no longer. "What'd you find last night, Christina?" she asked. "Was it a clue?"

Christina glanced around the restaurant. Glasses and silverware tinkled above the steady drone of conversation. Nobody seemed to be watching them. She reached into her sweater and thumped the folded piece of paper across the table like a paper football.

Julie opened it gently and read it to Grant and Jim:

> *If you're so smart,*
> *follow the V's—low like*
> *Minnesota's namesake,*
> *then high above the trees.*

11
MIMI HAHA

Papa's friend Chester opened the door for Mimi and helped her inside the SUV as if she were a movie star. "It's not often I get to chauffeur a famous author around the Twin Cities," he said.

Julie and Jim had followed Christina and Grant outside to see them off. "I wish—" Christina wanted to say she wished Julie and Jim could come along, but before she could finish her sentence, Papa cut her off.

"Why are you kids fiddlin' around?" Papa asked. "Scoot a boot on in the backseat."

"What do you mean?" Julie asked.

"I cleared it with your dad," Papa answered. "He and your mom are taking the dog team out for a run. They said you'd probably enjoy spending the day with our scalawags!"

"We sure would!" Jim said.

Christina grinned. "You took the words out of my mouth, Papa!" Once the SUV hit the road, the grownups talked loudly enough for the kids to whisper in secrecy.

"What do you think the clue means?" Julie asked Christina.

"I read a lot about Minnesota before we came," Christina said. "I remember learning that Minnesota is nicknamed the Gopher State. Maybe that's what the note meant by 'Minnesota's namesake.'"

"That's right," Julie said. "I didn't think of that!"

"That's as far as I've gotten with it," Christina said. "Unless we see some V's to follow, I'm at a dead end. What bothers me most though, is the way it's written—'If you're so smart.' Something about that gives me the willies. It's like someone is watching us!"

"Don't forget about 'Creepy' Karpis," Jim said.

"Thanks for reminding me about that!" Christina said sarcastically.

Christina looked at Grant, whose lips were still unnaturally rosy. He was unusually quiet. "What's wrong?" Christina asked. "Cat got your tongue?"

"No!" Jim blurted. "Lucy's got his lips!"

"'Unny Jim," Grant said. He touched his lips gingerly. "Some of the consonants hu't."

Christina, Jim, and Julie snickered, but Grant heard a loud "HA HA" come from the front of the SUV. He leaned forward so the grownups could hear and said, "It's not 'UNNY!"

"Oh, Grant," Mimi said. "We're not laughing at you! Chester was telling us about the falls."

"What falls?" Christina asked.

"Minnehaha Falls," Mimi replied. "Or as Grant would say, MIMI-Haha Falls."

The SUV rolled to a stop. "Here we are!" Chester said. "Minnehaha Falls, one of the oldest state parks in the country!"

"Is Minnehaha an Indian word?" Christina asked.

"It sure is," Chester replied. "Some people say it's the Indian word for 'laughing waters' because it has 'haha' on the end, but most believe it comes from a Dakota Indian word for waterfall."

"'Unny," said Grant. "I don't hear any water."

"Think about the time of year, Grant," Mimi said.

"You mean the falls are frozen?" Christina asked.

What should have been flowing water was frozen into thick columns of ice.

"Yes," said Shirley. "But I think it's even more beautiful now than in summer."

"Cool!" Grant said.

"Sure it's cool," Christina said. "It's ice!"

"If you want to see something really cool, follow me," Chester suggested.

The group eagerly traipsed behind Chester down a path that led directly to a shallow cave behind the falls. The sunlight shining through the frozen flow glowed a stunning azure blue.

Plink! Plink! Plink! "Listen carefully," Papa said. "You can hear water tinkling inside the columns of ice!" Peering through the bars of shiny frozen water, the kids could see that the creek below was a solid sheet of snow-covered ice.

Grant, still nursing his frostbitten lips, thought the frozen columns of ice looked like dinosaur teeth. "This 'eels like 'eing inside the mouth of a T-Wex," he said.

Mimi was about to agree with Grant's comparison when her red high heel caught on a small stone sticking up through the ground. Only Mimi would wear high heels on a hike through a park!

"That's righhhhhhhhhhhhhhhhhhhhhht!" she said as she slipped down an ice-covered path all the way to the frozen creek below.

The group stood dumbfounded until Mimi finally skidded to a halt. Her red knit hat was barely hanging on her right ear and her short blonde hair was waving crazily from static electricity.

"You OK?" Papa called down nervously.

Mimi gave two thumbs up and called back, "Just a little **abrasion** on my shin!"

Christina and Grant exploded with laughter. "I guess we really can call this Mimi-HaHa Falls now," Christina said between giggles.

"More like Mimi-Hahahahahahahaha!" Grant chortled. "But since Mimi blazed the twail, why don't we give it a twy!"

Grant tucked his coat under his bottom and plopped down onto the icy trail. "Weeeeeeeeee!" he shrieked all the way down. One by one, the group slid down until they all lay in a giggling heap.

"I don't know about everyone else," Papa said, "but my sittin' parts are cold!"

"Mine too," Mimi agreed. "I could sure go for some steaming hot chocolate!"

"I know a great little place in Minneapolis," Chester assured them. "That'll be our next stop!"

"Wooo!" Christina yelped. "Wooo... wooo....wooo!"

"Wow!" Jim said. "I've never seen anyone so excited about hot chocolate!"

"No!" Christina shouted, leaping to her feet and rubbing her backside. "It's not the hot chocolate. Something just bit my bottom!"

Sure enough, the snow where Christina had sat was crumbling up into a little pile. "I think something's moving under there!" Julie said.

"It's a giant worm!" Grant said as something pink wriggled up through the snow.

"It's a rat!" Christina shrieked as a black furry head surfaced.

"It's a starnose mole!" Chester said as two flippered feet flapped out onto the snow. "Poor little guy. He must have lost his way. Those tentacles sticking out from his nose help him find worms in the tunnels he makes."

"He made an honest mistake," Grant said. "Christina does look kinda wormy!"

Grant waited for Christina's comeback, but instead saw a faraway look in her eyes. It was the look she got when her mind was working warp speed—warp speed on the solution to a clue!

12
GOPHER GRAFFITI

Christina stared through the SUV's sunroof at the blue ribbon of sky running between the skyscrapers. "Are we in Minneapolis yet?" she asked.

"We passed the Minneapolis city limits sign a few minutes ago," Mimi answered.

"It doesn't look much different from Saint Paul," Grant said. "I guess the Twin Cities are identical twins."

"They have a lot in common," Mimi said. "But each is a unique city with its own government."

"Yes," Chester agreed. "You might say both cities share the same mother—the Mississippi River. Saint Paul was born as a river landing. It was a natural place for people who traveled on the river to stop and rest. From that it grew into a trading center."

"Minneapolis was known more for its industry, right?" Mimi asked.

"That's right," Chester said. "Minneapolis got its start thanks to Saint Anthony Falls. It's the only natural waterfall on the upper Mississippi."

"Oh, I get it," Christina said. "They used the waterfall to generate power to run machines."

"Exactly!" Chester said. "Waterfall power ran sawmills and flour mills."

"You mean they made plastic 'owahs?" Grant asked.

"Oh, Grant!" Christina said. "Will your lips ever get well enough to say 'f's' again? He's not talking about plastic flowers. He means the kind of flour that's used to make bread."

"And doughnuts!" Papa added. "In fact, I can almost smell doughnuts right now!"

"That's your imagination," Chester said with a chuckle. "But the little place I'm taking you to has the best doughnuts and hot chocolate in Minneapolis."

Suddenly, the SUV's sunroof went dark. "Hey!" Grant shouted. "Who turned out the lights?"

"No worries, Grant," Mimi said. "We're going through a tunnel."

Dim, sickly-green lights flashed by the SUV windows. The seed of an idea planted when Christina saw the mole pop out of the snow was taking root. "Julie," she whispered.

"Moles live in tunnels, right?"

"Sure," Julie whispered back.

"Gophers live in tunnels too!" Christina said. "Remember, the clue said 'low like Minnesota's namesake'—the gopher. I think it was talking about a tunnel! We better start looking for V's to follow right now!"

The girls told the boys to help scan the tunnel walls. It didn't take long for Grant and Christina to spot a big black V spray-painted inside a red circle.

Grant, still having lip problems, had difficulty saying the letter. "E!" he shouted. At the same time Christina shouted, "V!"

Mimi, clueless about their discovery, put the letters together. "Who's Evie?" she asked. "Did you see graffiti of that name? It's a shame when people deface public property."

"It's illegal too," Shirley agreed.

For the kids, graffiti was the least of their worries. "At least we know we're going in the right direction," Christina whispered. "It's almost like the person who left the clue knew we'd be coming through here. But how is that possible? I told you I feel like someone is watching us!"

13

SKYWAY HIGHWAY

The SUV snaked its way through a parking deck. When it finally stopped, the kids scrambled out, eager for the hot chocolate Chester had promised.

Christina looked at the city streets below. Cars drove by, but the sidewalks were eerily empty. "Where are all the people?" she asked. "It's like everyone disappeared."

"It's t-t-too c-c-cold for people to be out," Grant said, pulling his coat collar up around his neck.

"It often is," Shirley said. "That's why both Saint Paul and Minneapolis have skyway systems."

"Skyway systems?" Grant asked.

"It's a way for people to get around the city without being outside," Chester explained. "The Minneapolis skyway system is more than eight miles long."

Seeing the confused look on Grant's face, Chester said, "Come on, I'll show you."

The parking garage elevator took them up two floors and they exited into a long hallway lined with windows from floor to ceiling. The city's skyscrapers towered outside. Grant pressed his nose to the glass. "We're right over a street!" he said.

"The skyways are like covered bridges between the buildings," Mimi said. "Sure beats walking on the cold sidewalks!"

The kids raced down the skyway ahead of the adults. "I won!" Grant hollered. His voice echoed as if he was in a cave.

Christina looked at the sidewalk beneath them and realized she could see the top of a leafless tree. "This is it!" she said. "We're on the right track! The last part of the clue said to follow the V's high above the trees. We need to look for more V's in the skyway system!"

"Could we please look for the doughnuts first?" Grant pleaded.

"Yes," Christina said, "but we can keep our eyes open along the way. At least I can tell your lips are feeling better. I heard an 'f' in your sentence!"

"V's and F's," Grant said. "This mystery is like a bowl of alphabet soup!"

The kids crossed above two more streets inside the skyways before they reached the bakery Chester had promised. He hadn't exaggerated.

Christina felt every swallow of the rich, creamy hot chocolate go down, down, down her throat like a warm elevator headed for her stomach. "I feel like I've got a warm and fuzzy blanket on the inside," she told Chester.

The doughnuts were just as amazing. Every bite shattered the sugar glaze and revealed the chewy center.

"This area is known for its twins," Grant said when he'd finished his first doughnut. "So I think we should all get twin doughnuts!"

"Great idea, Grant!" Papa agreed.

By the time the kids finished their doughnuts, Papa and Mimi had ordered four more—quadruplets! But Christina was restless. "Mimi, can we look around while you finish your doughnuts?" she asked.

Mimi sipped hot chocolate to wash down a mouthful of doughnut before she replied. "Take my phone," she said, handing Christina her red, crystal-crusted cell phone. "Meet us back here in 30 minutes."

The kids ambled past boutiques, restaurants, and offices that opened onto the skyway. A man dressed in a short-sleeve Hawaiian shirt and shorts strode briskly by.

"I guess he hasn't stuck his head outdoors in a while," Christina said.

"People who live in apartment buildings that connect to the skyway never have to go outside," Julie said. "They have everything they need indoors."

"I'd feel like a pet hamster running around one of those plastic tubes," Grant said. "I sure hope we don't have to run inside a wheel."

Suddenly, something lying on the floor near an elevator captured Christina's eye. She sprinted to it for a closer look. "Look at this!" she said, holding up a pair of black goggles. "These are just like the ones the Vulcan Krewe guy wore in the hotel lobby."

"The person you saw drop the first note?" Grant asked.

"Yes!" Christina said as she shifted her gaze to a backlit map of the skyway system shining on the wall. "I don't believe it—looks like he drew a black V on the map! He had to remove the goggles so he could see how to write on the map. He's telling us where to find our next clue!"

"What is this person's obsession with V's?" Grant asked.

"The Vulcan Krewe members draw V's on the cheeks or foreheads of those who agree to support Vulcanus Rex, the Fire King, and to forsake the King of the Winds, King Boreas," Julie said. "Maybe this is someone who wants to mark us for Vulcanus Rex."

Grant struck a super-hero pose. "Never!" he said in a deep, melodramatic voice. "I want to follow King Boreas and have a blast at the Winter Carnival!"

"There's only one way we can know for sure," Christina said. She tapped the map and drew an imaginary trail with her finger. "We need to get here. Let's go!"

With their feet making dull thuds on the carpeted skyway floors, the kids galloped toward the area marked on the map, dodging other travelers along the way. "It should be just ahead," Christina said, pushing hard on a heavy glass door that separated the skywalk from an apartment building.

Three hallways branched off a small, circular lobby. Christina surveyed the area. "Does anyone see anything that looks like a clue?" she asked.

"Nope!" Jim said.

"Nothing," Julie said, disappointed.

Grant was feeling under a table. "Got it!" he said.

The others hovered around him. "What is it?" Christina asked expectantly.

Grant slowly pulled his hand out. "Oh, gross!" he groaned. A sticky wad of pink bubble gum formed a web between his fingers.

"Congratulations!" Jim said sarcastically.

"Maybe we came too far," Christina suggested as she pushed back through the glass doors. Then, she noticed it almost immediately. "How did we miss that?" she said, pointing to a fogged portion of the skyway glass.

In a cloudlike circle formed by hot breath on the glass was the clue the kids were searching for:

Up and down, round and round, behind the looking glass is where it's found.

14
RED RUNNING SUIT RUNS

Christina peered through the clear letters someone had scrawled in the condensation. The Minneapolis skyscrapers stood tall and strong all around them. But inside she felt small and inadequate. Sure, they had found several clues rather easily— almost too easily. But where had the clues gotten them? The Winter Carnival was set to begin the next day and they were no closer to finding the stolen medallion.

"Is that spit?" Grant asked as a drop of water ran down from the clue and splashed on a metal handrail.

"Yuck, no!" Christina said. "But whoever left this clue came through here right before us. I'm surprised we didn't catch him writing it."

The thought frightened Christina, who jumped when Mimi's phone buzzed in her pocket. "Uh-oh!" she said, realizing they'd been gone more than the promised 30 minutes.

Mimi and Papa, Chester and Shirley were lingering over their hot chocolate when the kids returned. "Too bad you took so long," Mimi said. "You could've met Chester and Shirley's young friend Mark."

"Remember I told you about the twin boys of our next-door neighbor?" Chester said. "Mark is one of them. He recently got his first job as a reporter for the Saint Paul newspaper and rented an apartment here in Minneapolis."

"You mean they let a kid rent an apartment?" Grant asked. "If I had my own apartment, I'd eat cold pizza for breakfast, cereal for lunch, and peanut butter and jelly sandwiches for supper—yum!"

Papa laughed at his silly grandson. "You'd have more than your own apartment," he said. "You'd also have a big bellyache."

"Mark isn't a kid anymore," Chester explained. "He's 22 years old!"

"I really miss them being kids," Shirley added. "We enjoyed being part of their lives as they grew up. We felt like we were their second set of parents."

"Does Mark's twin brother work at the paper too?" Christina asked.

Chester knitted his brows and swirled the last bit of hot chocolate in his cup. "Matthew hasn't decided what he's going to do with his life," he said. "He's been taking odd jobs until he finds something he likes."

Christina could tell Chester was concerned about his young friend. "Are they identical?" she asked.

Chester chuckled. "A lot of people can't tell them apart," he said. "It took us years, but it's easier now. Mark loves to dress up and Matthew is a bit of a slob. He prefers baggy sweats to a suit and tie."

Mimi, who had been perusing a newspaper, suddenly snickered. "This is hilarious!" she said.

"What is it, Mimi?" Christina asked.

"Says here," Mimi explained, "that a member of the Vulcan Krewe wore his red running suit to the gym. When he took it off to take a shower, someone stole it! He had to drive home in a towel!"

Papa slapped his knee. "Well, it was a running suit," he said. "Maybe it ran away!"

The adults shared a good laugh, but the kids just looked at each other. *Could the running suit thief be the same person leaving them clues?*

15
MEGA MALL

"Who's ready to shop for parkas?" Chester asked.

"Parkas?" Grant asked.

"If I'm taking you ice fishing tomorrow, you need heavy parkas to wear," Chester replied.

"Ice fishing!" Grant said excitedly. "Really?"

"Really!" Chester promised.

"I love fishing," Grant said, "but I hate shopping!"

"This is one shopping trip you'll love," Mimi promised. "You've never seen a shopping mall like Mall of America. It's the largest shopping mall in the United States!"

"Is it here in Minneapolis?" Christina asked.

"No," Mimi replied. "It's in Bloomington."

"It's only a 15-minute ride by train," Chester said.

When they arrived at the Mall of America, Grant was still concerned. "This place looks humongous," he said to Papa. "We'll never get Mimi and Christina out of there!"

"We'll see," Papa said. "We may never get you out of there!"

"Are you kidding?" Grant asked. "I hate shopping malls!"

Papa watched Grant carefully as they entered the mall under the bright red, white and blue, star-studded sign. He was like a kid in shock. "I think Chester made a mistake!" Grant said. "This isn't a shopping mall, it's an amusement park!"

"No mistake, Grant," Chester said. "It really is a shopping mall, but it also has one of the world's largest indoor amusement parks. About 40 million people come here each year."

For once, Grant was speechless. If he'd felt like a hamster in the Minneapolis skyway system, he felt like an ant inside a kid's ant farm now! The sun glared down through a clear ceiling to warm the bustling mall. Thousands of shoppers milled among four floors stacked like the layers of Mimi's coconut cake. And in the center, roller coasters filled with screamers zipped up to the ceiling, then down and around on the floor, while logs splashed down a log ride flume, a sparkling Ferris wheel turned merrily, and acres of other attractions battled for Grant's attention. Bells clanged, buzzers buzzed, and lights of every color in the rainbow winked and flashed flirtatiously.

Finally, Grant spoke. "You may call this a shopping mall," he said. "But I call it heaven!"

Christina was equally impressed. "Yeah!" she agreed.

"You haven't seen anything yet," Jim said. "There's even an aquarium with real sharks!"

"Can we explore before we shop?" Christina begged.

"Sure," Mimi said. "I know your sizes, so I'll pick out some parkas for you. You both wanted pink, right?" She winked at Christina.

"Oh, Mimi," Grant said. "Do I have to tell you again? Any color except pink or purple." He quickly realized he might have insulted Jim and Julie, who were wearing their purple parkas. "No offense guys," he said. "Just not my colors."

"That's OK," Julie said. "We wouldn't want to look like quadruplets!"

Mimi gave the kids the same speech she gave every time they were going to be out of her sight. "Here's my phone. Stay together and don't talk to strangers!"

The adults had already set out for a department store when Christina realized she'd forgotten something. "Wait!" she called. "Are the rides free?"

Without saying a word, Papa pulled out his black leather wallet. "Don't spend it all in one place," he cautioned as he counted bills out into each outstretched hand.

"Buy yourselves some lunch!" Mimi added.

When the adults were out of earshot, Grant raised his arms in the air and shouted, "Let's ride!"

"No!" Christina scolded. "We're not **amateur** sleuths. We've got a mystery to solve."

"What do you think I'm doing?" Grant asked. "The clue said 'up and down, round and round.' Don't you think that describes a roller coaster?"

"It could be," Christina said. "But I'm not even sure the answer to the clue is at the mall. If it is, I'll know for sure someone is watching our every move. It's just too much of a coincidence that the answers to clues always seem to appear at the places we go."

"The sharks go up and down and round and round," Jim said. "Why don't we start there?"

"Your idea is as good as Grant's," Christina said, clicking her teeth together in a ferocious grin. "The sharks it is!"

The kids entered a long, clear tunnel beneath the Underwater Adventure Aquarium. Christina felt apprehensive. They were a long way from Mimi and Papa, she feared someone was watching them, and here they were in a tube—under a gigantic mall, under the earth, under millions of gallons of water and under man-eating sharks! If someone wanted to trap them, this would be the place to do it!

"I was just thinking," Julie said. "Inside a shark tank would be a great place to hide something."

"Like a stolen medallion?" Christina asked. "Let's start looking for clues."

"It's gonna take a while," Julie said. "This is the world's largest underground aquarium."

"Everything here is super-sized, isn't it?" Christina remarked.

The sharks swam above them like deadly submarines. One of them seemed to be following Grant. "He's watching me with those dead eyes," Grant said. "I hope he's not hankerin' for a Grant burger."

Suddenly, a big dead fish floated down through the water. SMACK! The shark lunged and bit the fish in half. Its severed head came to rest on the tube above Grant's head. "Whew!" Grant said with a shudder. "That could have been me!"

The kids stopped at a tank filled with all shapes and sizes of jellyfish that wafted through the water like **lithe** ghosts.

"Look!" Christina said. "They're going up and down and round and round," she said.

"The clue also said something about 'behind the looking glass,'" Julie added as she tapped the glass. "Could this be it?"

"Please don't tap the glass!" an aquarium attendant said sternly.

Julie blushed. "Sorry," she said sheepishly.

Reflected in the tank's glass, Julie's embarrassed face was not the only red thing that Christina saw. Lurking behind them was someone wearing red—a red running suit!

16
HEAD OVER HEELS

No one else had seen the reflection of the red running suit. Grant thought Christina was being paranoid. "Are you sure it wasn't your imagination?" he asked, proud that he wasn't the one being accused of an overactive imagination for once.

Although she had doubts about whether they were chasing someone in a red running suit or if someone in a red running suit was chasing them, Christina knew what she had seen. "No doubt about it!" she exclaimed, her heart still pounding.

"Since the aquarium didn't have any clues," Jim said, "where do we go next?"

"Last one on a roller coaster is shark bait!" Grant yelled.

When the attendant buckled them into the Rock Bottom Plunge Roller Coaster in the Nickelodeon Universe amusement park, Christina knew it was too late to back out. She didn't share her brother's love of all things fast and furious, turbo and twisty. "I hope I don't get sick," she said, nervously combing her hair back with her fingers.

"One thing's for sure," Grant said. "This one definitely goes up and down and round and round. It's gonna be awesome!" He pumped his scrawny arm in the air.

Christina glanced at her fellow passengers. Two teenagers sitting beside her bragged about how many times they had "survived" the Rock Bottom Plunge. When she looked at the row of seats behind her, however, her first instinct was to unbuckle and jump out! A man in complete Vulcan Krewe garb waved a gloved hand at her!

Christina gulped and poked Julie in the side. "We've got to get out of here," she whispered frantically. "Look behind us!"

Julie looked behind and then back at Christina who was fumbling with her seat buckle.

"Christina, you can't!" Julie cautioned as a warning bell blew. "The roller coaster is moving!"

"I'm calling Mimi and Papa!" Christina said as she dug in her pocket for Mimi's cell phone.

The roller coaster started its ascent, climbing and creaking slowly up the incline. It gradually accelerated until Christina's hair was flying behind her head. Her fingers got hold of Mimi's phone just as the coaster sped into a spiral. Suddenly they were head over heels!

"Oh, nooooooo!" Christina yelled as she watched Mimi's phone fly by her face. She tried to see it but the coaster's speed made her eyes water. She could only imagine Mimi's phone shattered in thousands of pieces on the mall floor!

"Weeeee!" Grant squealed with joy.

But Christina just squeezed her eyes closed and wished for the coaster to stop. When she felt it slowing down, she was relieved and opened her eyes. Unfortunately, it was just in time to see "the plunge."

"Hold on tight, Christina!" Julie shouted.

"No!" Grant shouted. "Let's all raise our arms in the air!"

Christina's sweaty hands squeezed the safety bar even tighter. She felt her stomach turn somersaults like a kid on the first day of spring break. The coaster plunged at breakneck speed back down to the mall floor.

"Juuuuump ouuuuuuut wheeeeeeen weeeeeee stoooop!" Christina yelled.

When the coaster finally stopped, Christina glanced again over her shoulder at the Vulcan Krewe member. Goggles and the red hood blocked his face, but Christina could tell he was sneering. He raised a victorious fist in the air and jumped out of his seat ahead of the kids. To Christina's amazement, he joined three other Krewe members waiting for him.

"I guess you were right about seeing the red running suit at the aquarium," Grant said. "It looks like there are lots of Krewe members at the mall today."

Great! Christina thought. *How will we ever find out who our clue dropper is?*

17
MIRROR, MIRROR ON THE WALL

"Got it!" Grant shouted as he shimmied down one of trees growing contentedly in the amusement park. He wondered if the lush trees, plants, and flowers inside the mall had any idea that outside the mall, other living things were frozen under a blanket of snow.

Christina was certainly happy the vegetation was there. One of the trees was gently cradling Mimi's cell phone in its branches. The kids spotted it when they heard it ringing with Mimi's special ring tone—a show tune performed by the Atlanta Symphony Orchestra.

"That's either Mimi's cell phone, or there are some crazy birds in this place," Christina had said.

Mimi was just checking to make sure they were safe and having a good time. She had no idea that her phone had just taken the thrill ride of a lifetime! After the kids grabbed a quick burger and fries at the food court, they sauntered through the other mall attractions.

"Hey, why don't we play hide and seek?" Jim suggested.

"We could find good places to hide," Grant said. "But I'm afraid we'd never find each other."

"And we promised Mimi we'd stay together," Christina reminded them.

"I know what Jim's thinking," Julie said. "The Amazing Mirror Maze."

"Yeah!" Jim said. "We could play hide and seek and be in the same place."

Grant rubbed his lips. "There aren't any girls in it, are there?" he asked.

Julie and Jim chuckled. "No girls," Jim promised. "At least no freezing cold, metal ones."

When they reached the Mirror Maze and bought their tickets, they had to pull on plastic gloves before they gained **access**. "Keeps fingerprints off the mirrors," the attendant told them.

The maze was unlike anything Christina had ever seen. Arches adorned with colorful diamond shapes framed the hallways lined with glass and mirrors. Colorful laser lights pierced the darkness and ricocheted off the mirrors in every direction. Jim quickly trotted down one of the hallways and disappeared. Grant tried to follow, but WHAP, he ran right into a mirror. "First my lips and now my forehead!" he moaned as he rubbed a growing goose egg.

"Catch me if you can!" Julie teased as she left Christina standing all alone.

Christina looked down a hallway only to see hundreds of Christinas looking back at her. *This is so weird*, she thought. *I feel like I'm inside a disco ball.*

Then Christina realized something. *Another word for mirror is looking glass!* she thought. *This could be the answer to the clue! We went round and round and up and down and now we're in the perfect place to look behind the looking glass!*

Christina wanted to share her revelation with the others, but they were nowhere in sight. She shuffled down a corridor with her gloved hands outstretched to keep from running into a mirror.

"Grant?" she called when she saw a boy run in front of her. But when she reached out her hand, it was only a reflection from somewhere behind her. Christina felt all around the mirror. There seemed to be no way to get to the back of that mirror or any of the others in the maze. She continued until she found herself at a dead end. With only a purple band of light glowing in the black ceiling, she could barely see her own reflection, much less the way out.

Christina felt along the mirrored wall like a trapped mole—until she saw a familiar form reflected behind her. Even in the dim light, she could tell it was a red running suit! Her heart pounded and she spun on her heels to face the mysterious figure.

"Are you following me?" she asked. There was no answer. It was still only a reflection. Christina slowly turned in every direction. At least a dozen men in red running suits surrounded her, but all of them seemed to be reflections. Was there really a dozen of them, or only one?

She grabbed in her pocket for Mimi's phone when she realized that Grant still had it! Then, all the mouths in the reflected faces moved at once. "If you're so smart," a raspy voice said. "Mind your own business!"

18
FISHY FIST

"ChrisTEENAA," Grant yelled. "Mimi called! It's time to go!" Christina had never been so relieved to hear her pesky little brother yell her name.

As quickly as the reflected image of the man in the red running suit had appeared, it disappeared. Christina whirled around, looking in every direction to see if she could make out where the real person was, but could see no one.

"Here, Grant," she yelled back to her little brother. "Hurry!"

All four kids played Marco Polo in the maze until they met at the entrance. "OK, that's my new favorite place," Grant said. "That was awesome!"

"I would describe it as terrifying," Christina said, then shared her story of the man in the red running suit. "I just don't understand what he's up to."

"How do you know it's the clue dropper?" Julie asked. "There were a lot of Vulcans in the mall today."

"Remember the clue that said, 'If you're so smart...?'" Christina asked. "He said, 'if you're so smart, mind your own business.' It has to be him!"

Just as Papa predicted, Grant wanted to spend more time at the mall when it was time to leave.

"My dogs are killing me!" Papa said. "And I'm ready to find some good Minnesota grub."

Mimi held up two hefty shopping bags, "As you can see, we got what we came for."

"Oh!" Christina cried. "Can we see our parkas?"

Mimi opened a bag and pulled out a puffy red parka with a fake fur-trimmed hood.

"Red?" Christina said. "I should've known! I hope no one mistakes me for a Vulcan Krewe member."

"Is mine red too?" Grant asked.

"What else?" Mimi answered. "This way you can pretend to be twins and you'll be easy to spot in the snow."

That's what I'm afraid of, Christina thought.

Back in Saint Paul, Chester chose a restaurant specializing in Minnesota foods. "I'd like to order for you," he said. "I want you to try a traditional winter Minnesota dish."

Grant prayed it was pepperoni pizza. He was surprised instead with a large white blob served with boiled potatoes and green peas. He crinkled his nose at the unappetizing combo. "What is this?" he asked. "It smells kinda fishy."

"It's lutefisk," Chester said.

"Disgusting!" Grant cried. "Who is Lute and why would I want to eat his fist?"

Christina knew Grant's understanding of the word was probably wrong. But she agreed about the disgusting part. Mimi was mortified that Grant had called Chester's food selection disgusting before he even tasted it.

After chuckling at Grant's misunderstanding, Chester explained, "Many of the first immigrants to Minnesota were from the Nordic countries of Europe, such as Sweden and Norway. They had to dry fish to preserve it for the cold winter months. Then, they soaked the dry fish in a solution made with lye to plump it back up to its original shape."

"Sort of like those tiny animal-shaped sponges that grow big when you put them in water?" Grant asked.

"Exactly," Chester said. "Now go on and give it a try!"

Grant speared a piece of lutefisk with his fork and lifted it to his lips with apprehension. Christina, Jim, and Julie watched his reaction before they tried theirs. Grant smacked as if trying to find an accurate description for the flavor.

"Hmmm...," he said, "tastes like fish-flavored Jell-O." Without missing a beat, he quickly added, "Papa, could we have pepperoni pizza for dessert?"

For the rest of the meal, the kids ate their potatoes and peas, but pushed the lutefisk around on their plates. They hoped Papa would come through with the pizza later.

Mimi had excused herself to go to the restroom. After she was gone for what seemed like forever, Christina grew worried. She was about to check on Mimi when an announcer's voice boomed in the restaurant: "Ladies and gentlemen! For this evening's entertainment, please turn your attention to the stage. Welcome some special visitors from Saint Paul's Winter Carnival—this year's beautiful crop of Klondike Kates!"

About a dozen women stepped onto the stage. They wore all sorts of flashy, fancy red and black costumes adorned with sequins, feather headdresses, and boas.

"Who's Klondike Kate?" Christina asked.

"She was a famous dance hall girl in the northern regions, including Minnesota, during the Gold Rush era of the late 1800s," Shirley explained. "The miners made her rich by giving her gold nuggets and gold dust. Now, women are chosen each year to dress up as Klondike Kate and act as entertainers for the Winter Carnival."

Christina watched the women sing and twirl. Suddenly she noticed a Klondike Kate on the back row who was not kicking quite as high as the others. She blinked hard and looked again. *No, it couldn't be*, she thought. *Mimi?!*

Mimi returned to the table breathless, but glowing in her Klondike Kate outfit. "One of the Kate's got sick and had to leave," she explained. "I happened to be in the restroom and you know how good I look in red! They even invited me to participate in the Carnival opening ceremonies tomorrow night!"

Chester suddenly waved at someone across the room. "Mark!" he shouted. A young man in a business suit was skirting around the back wall of the restaurant. "Oh, well," Chester said. "Guess he didn't see me."

Christina spun in her seat to get a look at Mark. There were several men walking around the restaurant in suits. And one of them looked an awful lot like the man they had seen frantically searching for something in the hotel lobby!

19
LITTLE FISHING HUT ON THE LAKE

The morning was clear and the air so crisp, Christina felt it might shatter if she tapped it with a hammer. They had loaded the SUV before daybreak and had the pleasure of watching the sunrise as they drove to one of Saint Paul's many sparkling lakes.

"Minnesota is a beautiful state!" Christina said.

"I can't wait to write about it," Mimi agreed. "With Minnesota's 10,000 lakes, it's easy to understand how the Dakota Indians chose the name."

"The Indians named it?" Grant asked.

Mimi had already done her research. "In the Dakota language, *minne* means water and *sotah* means the color of the sky."

Christina was glad Julie and Jim had gotten permission to come along. Time was running out to find the missing medallion before the Winter Carnival opening ceremonies that night!

During the short ride, Christina thought of Laura Ingalls Wilder, author of *Little House on the Prairie* and other books about frontier life. Laura Ingalls Wilder had to get up on cold mornings like this one to do her chores. She wrote *On the Banks of Plum Creek* based on a part of her childhood lived near Walnut Grove, Minnesota. After Mimi, she was Christina's favorite author.

"Is that an Indian village?" Grant asked when they arrived. Small huts that resembled tepees dotted what appeared to be a field covered in snow.

"Those are fishing huts," Chester explained.

"But where's the lake?" Grant asked.

"You're standing on it!" Papa said.

"You mean there are fish swimming under our feet right now?" Grant asked.

"I sure hope so!" Chester said as he unpacked their gear. "Big, fat walleyes!"

"Walleyes?" Christina asked.

"That's what we usually fish for in Minnesota," Chester said. "But we'll take anything that jumps on our hook!"

Christina's teeth chattered as the biting wind gnawed its way through her thick parka. The frosty vapor of her breath grabbed the fur around her hood and formed sparkling ice crystals. The icy cold crept up through the soles of her boots. "It feels like someone is sticking pins in my feet!" she said, stomping the ice.

"It'll be warmer when we get the hut up," Chester promised.

He cranked an ice auger to drill several holes through the thick ice. It reminded Christina of a giant drill that sounded like a lawn mower. A ring of crushed ice soon surrounded a hole like a frosty doughnut. Inside was the dark lake water. Chester lowered a metal ladle with holes in it into the fishing hole to keep it from freezing over.

Next, Papa helped Chester erect a fishing hut that resembled a camping tent over the hole. "This is cozier," Christina said, thankful to be out of the wind. "But I wish we could build a campfire."

Mimi laughed. "Fire melts ice, remember?" she said. "Maybe this will help." She poured hot chocolate for everyone from her big red thermos while Chester passed out the fishing rods.

"Hey!" Grant complained when he grabbed his rod. "Where's the rest of it?"

"Ice fishing rods are much shorter than regular rods," Papa explained. "You don't have to cast the line, just drop the lure into the hole."

Grant speared a sardine-sized bait fish as shiny as a new coin with his hook and plopped it into the fishing hole. Frigid droplets smacked Christina in the eye. "Watch it!" she said.

Within seconds Grant yelled, "He's got me!"

"Don't you mean you've got him?" Christina asked.

"N-n-noo!" Grant said, his feet starting to skid on the ice. He cranked the reel frantically, but fell to his knees as it bent into an arch. "Help!" he cried. Christina was about to grab him around the waist when Grant fell on his belly and slid up to the hole. Christina grabbed one of his feet, but not before his hands plunged into the icy water. "Pull!" Grant shouted. "I didn't know there were whales in this lake!"

Jim grabbed Grant's other foot and they pulled with all their might. Grant's hands came out of the fishing hole followed by an enormous, slimy, wet walleye!

"That's a keeper!" Chester shouted. "Throw it outside the tent to freeze solid before we take it home."

While everyone admired the fish's brown and green splotches and spiny fins, Christina fetched newspaper from Chester's bag to wrap it later. The comics section was on top and she couldn't resist pausing long enough to read *Peanuts*.

Christina could feel the blood drain from her face as she read the strip. In the first frame, Linus told Charlie Brown, "Lucy will tell you what to do!" In the second frame, Lucy said, "Don't put your dreams on ice, build your palace!" In the third frame, Charlie Brown built a castle out of tiny blocks he chipped from ice cubes. Crowning the top of the ice castle was a medallion!

Christina's brain was clicking faster than a computer. The clues, the people, the places—like a 1,000-piece puzzle, she was *finally* seeing the big picture. Trouble was, she didn't like what she saw—at all!

20
WALLEYED WILD RIDE

Barking dogs interrupted Christina's thoughts. She lifted a flap on the side of the fishing hut and saw Julie and Jim's dad, Mr. Snowdon, telling his lead dog, "Stay!"

"Do I smell hot chocolate?" Mr. Snowdon asked when he entered the hut.

Jim and Julie gave their dad a bear hug. "What are you doing here?" Jim asked.

"Just warming the dogs up for today's sled trials," he said. "Thought I'd pop in and see if the fish are biting."

Grant held his walleye above his head and grinned. "Yep!" he said.

Jim and Julie were eager for Christina and Grant to meet the sled team. "Dad, can I take the dogs for a spin?" Jim asked. "If I'm going to be a champion musher like you, I need the practice!"

"OK," Mr. Snowdon said. "But you know how they like to run. Don't get carried away!"

Twelve fluffy tails arching over the sled dogs' backs wagged happily when the kids went out to meet them. "They look a little like wolves," Grant said. "What kind of dogs are they?"

"Siberian Huskies," Julie said. "Look at their big feet. They were made for speed on the snow and ice."

Christina buried her fingers in the lead dog's dense fur and scratched his head. "What's this one's name?" she asked.

"Snoopy," Julie replied. "You know, like the *Peanuts* character."

Suddenly, Christina knew what she had to do, even though it would probably land them in a heap of trouble. She pulled the kids into a huddle and shared her bombshell news. "I know where the medallion is," she whispered mysteriously. "If we don't find it and turn it in to the officials by this afternoon, the medallion hunt will be canceled. Chester and Shirley won't have the chance to win the money they need to bring the twins home. We've got to get there fast!"

"Are you thinking what I'm thinking?" Jim asked.

Christina nodded slyly and hopped on the sled. The other kids joined her and Jim hollered, "MUSH!"

The dogs took off like a rifle shot across the frozen lake. They weaved among fishing huts and surprised fishermen with their tongues flapping happily out of the corners of their mouths.

Soon they were on a course the dogs had memorized like homing pigeons. Luckily, it led straight back to the grounds of the Winter Carnival. Snow and ice chips flew up from the sled's runners and pelted the kids, who hung on for dear life. Through parks, around trees, over hills and under bridges, Snoopy led the way with confidence.

Finally, Christina saw what she was looking for—four spires sparkling in the noonday sun. Each was topped with an American flag!

21
PALACE OF PERIL

"That must be it!" Christina shouted. She had read about the famous Winter Carnival ice palace built from ice cut out of area lakes, but this one was grander than she had expected. Made entirely of sparkling ice blocks, it looked like a fitting home for the pickiest storybook princess, or in this case, King Boreas. It gleamed like glass against the Saint Paul skyline.

Jim ordered Snoopy and the rest of the panting dog team to "Stay!"

"We've got to get inside the palace," Christina said. "That's where they've hidden the medallion!"

"Who?" Grant asked.

"I'll explain later," Christina said as she made a beeline for the castle.

Near the castle, artists used screaming chainsaws to sculpt giant ice blocks for the ice-carving competition. They created every kind of figure imagineable, from birds to cartoon characters. In preparation for an upcoming parade, floats flaunted their colors, the horns of high school bands blared, jugglers juggled, and carnival characters cavorted. The smell of hot dogs and funnel cakes floated over the snow to lure the sightseers milling about. Electricians ran wires and carpenters built platforms in preparation for the coronation ceremony for King Boreas and his royal court.

"Uh, oh!" Grant said. "Look at the guards. I don't think we can get inside the palace."

"Where there's a will, there's a way," Christina said as she headed to the back side of the crystal castle.

A security guard chatting with a tourist seemed like their best chance. The kids cowered behind a snow bank and Christina whispered, "See that hole in the back wall? When I count to three, make a run for it!"

The kids scurried to the hole like frightened mice. Christina hoped their parade of red and purple parkas wouldn't attract the guard's attention. They slipped inside and landed in a chaotic pile. "How awesome is this?" Grant asked. He craned his head back to marvel at the soaring ceiling of the colossal ice palace.

What little light that shone through the ice blocks was greenish blue. The blocks themselves, held together by mortar made of snow, creaked and crackled. The kids crept to the center spire. Metal spikes formed a ladder up its side. Electricians had used them to run the lights that would dance in time to music at night.

From her coat pocket, Christina pulled out the *Peanuts* cartoon she'd ripped from the paper. The medallion was drawn on the fourteenth block near the top of the spire. She counted up 14 blocks in the real spire and sure enough, that's where a ledge protruded.

"I've got to climb up there," Christina said. "There's no way around it."

"Oh no, you don't," Grant said. "You know 'monkey' is my middle name!"

Grant grabbed an ice-cold spike and pulled himself up. Slowly he climbed from spike to spike, making his way to the ledge. "Only one more step," he called down. He was straining to reach the final spike when suddenly his foot slipped. Grant was hanging by one gloved hand!

"Grant!" Christina screamed in horror.

Grant quickly pedaled the air until a foot caught one of the spikes. "Gotta keep it exciting!" he yelled. In one deft move, he pushed himself up towards the ledge and brushed it with his free hand.

A white plastic disc floated to the ice floor and spun on its side like a top. Christina stopped it with her boot, picked it up and read, "You Found It! Bring this medallion to the *Pioneer Press* building and exchange it for King Boreas' treasure."

"This is it!" Christina cried. "Let's get it to the officials!"

"Not so fast," a booming voice warned. "Since you're so smart, you know I can't let you do that."

A man in a red running suit stepped around the corner of the spire. "We tried to keep you occupied with all those phony clues," he growled. "We warned you to mind your own business. But you wouldn't give up, would you?"

"Phony clues?" Julie asked. "Just who are you?"

"It's one of Chester and Shirley's twin friends, Mark or Matthew," Christina answered before the man could.

The man removed his hood. "I'm Matthew," he said. "Mark developed the plan, but I did all the leg work." He moved ominously toward the kids. "And now," he said. "I've got to finish it."

Christina noticed sunlight suddenly slant into the palace. She knew it had to be coming through an opening. She also noticed Grant had just reached the bottom spike. It was their only opportunity! Christina hoped Grant would follow her lead. She cut her eyes at him and gave a slight nod toward the wall.

"Could we settle this with a snowball fight?" Christina asked Matthew.

"You wish!" Matthew said. "Besides, there's no snow in here."

Christina watched her little brother scrape a handful of snow from between two blocks and squeeze it in his palm.

"What about there?!" Christina screamed and pointed at Grant. Matthew spun around. SPLAT! Grant's snowball hit Matthew between the eyes. He staggered while Christina ordered, "Run for the light!"

When they reached the entrance to the palace, they ran smack dab into a security guard who'd heard their screams. "You kids are in a heap of trouble," he said. "No one's allowed in the castle!"

22

TWIN BABYSITTERS

When the dogsled didn't come back, Mr. Snowdon had followed the tracks all the way to the palace where he found the dog team waiting patiently. And when he found the kids in the custody of the security guard, he phoned Mimi and Papa. They received a hearty tongue lashing, but it was followed by a heap of hugs.

That night, at the King Boreas coronation ceremony, Christina apologized to Chester and Shirley. "I'm sorry we had to turn in your friends," she said.

"You had no choice," Chester said. "We're very disappointed in the boys and never dreamed they'd do anything like this."

"Why'd they do it?" Grant asked.

"The boys' father left them when they were very young," Chester explained. "When they heard of our plans to adopt the twins in Haiti, they felt like they'd lose us too. They thought if they stole the medallion, it would keep us from winning the prize money we needed for the adoption."

"Yes," Shirley agreed. "They couldn't understand that we would still love them just as much as we always have."

"What will happen to them?" Christina asked.

"I've already spoken with their lawyer," Chester said. "Since the medallion was found in time for the opening ceremonies, they might get off with probation and some counseling."

Julie was still confused. "What were all those clues about?" she asked.

Christina explained. "Mark gave Matthew a note with instructions on what to do with the medallion after he stole it from the newspaper office."

"The Lucy note?" Grant asked.

"That's right," Christina said. "They worked out a system of communicating through clues hidden in the *Peanuts* comic strip. When Matthew lost that first note, Mark quickly figured out that we were the ones who found it. I guess he saw me pick it up.

"He learned from Chester and Shirley," she continued, "that we were good at solving mysteries. He wanted to keep us busy with a trail of fake clues, so we wouldn't find the medallion."

"So he was the young man in the business suit searching for something?" Grant asked.

"Yes," Christina said. "And Matthew stole the Vulcan Krewe running suit. It kept him incognito. They followed our movements by talking with Chester and Shirley. If Grant hadn't caught that fish, I guess I never would have seen the real clue in the *Peanuts* cartoon strip."

Suddenly, music boomed and colorful lights danced inside the ice palace.

"Breathtaking!" Mimi exclaimed.

"Yeah," Grant agreed. "We almost got our breath taken in there for good!"

Christina was about to tell Grant no one would want his stinky breath when the flashing swords of royal guards on the stage caught their attention. The previous year's King Boreas stepped under the arch and called forth the man chosen as the new King Boreas. A tall, gray-haired man dressed in a peacock blue, military-style uniform stepped forward to receive a jewel-encrusted scepter and glittering gold crown. After a few remarks, the new king made an announcement.

"Will Christina and Grant please come to the stage?" he asked in a booming voice.

"What did he say?" Grant asked in disbelief. "Us? Oh, no! Are we in trouble?"

Christina gripped his hand tightly. "Let's go find out," she replied.

The king smiled as the kids joined him on the stage. "I proclaim you official residents of the realm of King Boreas," he said. "And here is your reward for finding the missing medallion!"

Grant flung his fists in the air in relief. Christina smiled and graciously accepted the crisp white envelope. The kids peered inside it and found a check for more money than they'd ever seen before!

Christina and Grant exchanged a smile. Both knew exactly what to do. They turned and gave the check to Chester and Shirley.

"Why, this is exactly what we need for the adoption!" Shirley said, wiping away tears.

"I don't know what to say," Chester said.

"Say you'll invite us back to the Twin Cities to babysit the twins!" Christina said.

"Hey, speak for yourself!" Grant exclaimed. "I'm some bigwig in the realm of King Boreas and I rule!"

Mimi tousled Grant's blonde curls. "Enjoy it now, kiddo," she said. "You'll be back doing dishes in Georgia before you know it!"

Now...go to
www.carolemarshmysteries.com
and...

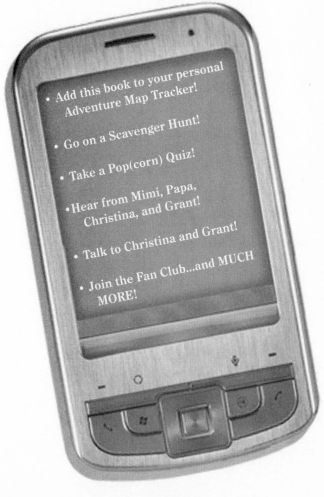

- Add this book to your personal Adventure Map Tracker!

- Go on a Scavenger Hunt!

- Take a Pop(corn) Quiz!

- Hear from Mimi, Papa, Christina, and Grant!

- Talk to Christina and Grant!

- Join the Fan Club...and MUCH MORE!

GLOSSARY

adoption: the act of taking the child of other parents as one's own child

azure: a shade of vivid blue

cavort: to leap or dance about in a lively manner

chauffeur: a person employed to drive a motor vehicle

gangster: a member of a gang of criminals

graffiti: unauthorized writing or drawing on a public surface

medallion: resembling a large medal

paranoid: extremely fearful

waft: to be driven or go lightly along, as by the air

abrasion: rubbing away by friction

access: permission or ability to enter

amateur: someone who doesn't have a lot of experience

lithe: easily bent

minutia: a minor detail

SAT GLOSSARY

abrasion: rubbing away by friction

access: permission or ability to enter

amateur: someone who doesn't have a lot of experience

lithe: easily bent

minutia: a minor detail

Enjoy this exciting excerpt from:

THE MYSTERY IN THE Smoky Mountains

1

FOLKLORE GALORE!

Christina looked up from her book and gazed out the airplane window. She felt the *Mystery Girl's* nose turn down for initial descent into the airport. It had been a short flight in the little airplane. It felt like they had just taken off!

"Gosh, Papa! That was fast!" Christina said to the pilot in a black cowboy hat, who also happened to be her grandfather.

"Uh, can you make it faster, please, Papa?" pleaded Grant, Christina's little brother. "I gotta go! Say, when are you gonna get a bathroom on this plane?"

Mimi giggled at her grandson squirming in his seat, his face twisted in discomfort. "Grant, I told you not to drink that sports drink before we left!" she said. She shut her shiny silver laptop computer and stuffed her red, sparkly mystery-writing glasses into her purse.

Mimi and Papa often brought their grandchildren, Christina and Grant, on research trips. Mimi wrote children's mystery books, and trips with her cowboy-pilot husband and her adventure-seeking grandkids were the best part of her job! This morning they traveled from Peachtree City, Georgia to Asheville, North Carolina, for Mimi to research folklore of the Great Smoky Mountains.

Christina yanked her long, brown hair into a quick ponytail and gazed out the window again. Mountains reached up to the clouds as far as she could see. Not the jagged, dark, rocky kind, but, rolling, tree-covered hills that stretched lazily toward the horizon. The autumn leaves on the trees created a collage of colors on the mountains—fiery orange, brick red, chestnut brown, and saffron yellow. Out of the corner of her eye, she spotted a plume of blue-grey smoke rising from the valleys between the mountain peaks.

"Grant, we'll stop at a bathroom as soon as we get to the airport, but you'll have to make it snappy!" said Papa. "We still have an hour drive to Penland School and we've got to get there by lunchtime."

"Wait, why are we going to a school?" asked Grant, shifting from side to side. "We're on fall break from our school. Why do we have to go to another one?"

"It's Penland School for Crafts, Grant," said Mimi. "Students of all ages come there to learn to make crafts and other beautiful works of art. It's the perfect place to start our travels through the Smoky Mountains."

"Well, as long as they're serving lunch, I'll go! I'm starved," said Grant.

"Typical!" said Christina. She leaned over to her brother and tousled his curly, blond hair.

The moment they landed at the Asheville airport and pulled into the hangar, Grant sprinted toward the nearest bathroom. Once he rejoined the group, the four travelers hopped into their rental car and Papa steered them toward Skyline Drive and the scenic trip north through Asheville.

In the back seat, Christina's stomach growled. She was so excited about the trip that morning, she didn't eat breakfast. She picked up her backpack and sifted through the contents. Maybe there's a leftover granola bar from school last week, she thought.

"Christina, grab your camera," said Mimi. "You'll want to take pictures of the scenery as we head through Asheville and up into the mountains. We've picked the best time of year to visit the Great Smokies!"

"We sure have," said Papa. "I love the canopy of autumn leaves and smell of the brisk fall air in these mountains!"

Instead of food, Christina pulled her camera from her backpack and began snapping pictures of the natural mountain beauty. Houses dotted the landscape, nestled within the trees and hills. Sometimes, faraway views peeked through the gorges that separated each mountaintop. Again she noticed wisps of white and blue-tinted smoke whirling up from the mountains.

The SUV circled up and around the side of a mountain, passing a slower car on the right. Suddenly, Grant's ears felt like they had filled with water. He felt pressure inside his head.

"Everything sounds weird in my head!" he yelped.

"It's OK, Grant!" said Christina. "Your ears are adjusting to the altitude of the mountains. Papa always says to swallow really hard and that will fix it."

Grant took a big gulp and the feeling in his ears returned to normal. Mimi and Papa gave each other a knowing glance. They were happy that their grandchildren actually remembered some of the helpful advice they had shared over the years!

"Kids, these mountains are filled with history and legend and folklore—galore!" said Mimi, adjusting the red ribbon on her wide-brimmed straw hat. "You only see orange and brown leaves and rocks and cliffs from the car, but when we visit the places I have planned for us, you'll be amazed at what you'll find! They don't call these the GREAT Smoky Mountains for nothing!"

Christina was about to ask Mimi if the smoke she saw rising from the mountains was the reason they were called the "Smoky Mountains," but Papa announced that they were almost at Penland School. That question would save for later.

Christina's stomach rumbled again. She caught Grant's attention and rubbed her belly. She wanted her brother to know that she was ready for lunch as much as he was! If only she had known what mysterious adventure would begin that day, she would have been sure to eat a healthy breakfast before she left home!

#
A PART OF A SECTION OF A WHOLE!

As Papa drove up the winding road to the school, Grant studied a map intently. Christina knew he was thinking hard because his tongue was sticking out of the side of his mouth and his face looked serious. Shaking the map in the air, Grant spoke. "Hey, what's going on here?" he said. "This map is trying to trick me. It says we're in three places at the same time!"

"Hmmm," said Mimi, turning to look at her grandson in the back seat. "That sounds like a mystery we need to solve!"

Grant handed Mimi his map. "See right here," he said, pointing to some gray triangles. "It says we are in the Appalachian Mountains *AND* the Blue Ridge Mountains *AND* the Great Smoky Mountains."

Papa pointed his index finger into the air. "This is no mystery, my boy," he said. "We are traveling right in the middle of a *part* of a *section* of a *whole*!"

Grant threw his hands on top of his head and shook it back and forth. "OK, now my head's going to explode!" he said. "A *what* of a *who* of a *how*?"

Papa explained, "The Appalachian Mountains are a *whole* mountain range, running from Alabama north to Canada. The Blue Ridge Mountains are a *section* of the Appalachian range, the eastern edge of the range, actually. The Great Smoky Mountains are *part* of the Blue Ridge Mountains. Specifically, they are the mountains along the North Carolina and Tennessee border."

It took a minute, but Grant's face lit up with understanding.

"Now I get it!" he declared. "It's just like eating pizza. I have a whole pizza. I take one section—that's the slice. Then I eat the anchovies first. The anchovies are a part of a section of a whole!"

"Ewwwww! Anchovies!" squealed Christina in disgust. How could her brother eat something so gross? No matter how hungry she was, she could NEVER eat anchovies!

Grant leaned over to his sister and licked his lips! "Mmmm mmmm good!!" he teased.

Trying to erase her annoying brother and oily fish parts from her mind, Christina peered out of the car window at the mountains in the distance. They looked like waves on the ocean, only with tints of orange and red instead of green and blue. More wisps of smoke caught her eye—lighter wisps this time.

"I guess the Smoky Mountains are named for all the smoke I've seen here," said Christina.

"Are the mountains on fire?" asked Grant. "Should we call the fire department, Papa?"

"No, my boy, it's not that kind of smoke," said Papa, pulling the car into a parking space. "It's actually a kind of mist. The warm air from the base of the mountains mixes with the cool air along the top of the mountains. That creates the smoke you see."

It was a perfectly beautiful day with a clear, blue sky, but the smoke added an eerie and mysterious feel to an otherwise **tranquil** setting. *Smoke, mist, fog—whatever you call it—I don't want to be in those mountains by myself,* thought Christina.